Freddie Fernortner

FEARLESS FIRST GRADER ®

Freddie   Darla   Chipper   Mr. Chewy

THE MAGICAL WADING POOL
BY JOHNATHAN RAND

An AudioCraft Publishing, Inc. book

Freddie Fernortner, Fearless First Grader
#7: The Magical Wading Pool
ISBN-13 digit: 978-1-893699-91-5

Illustrations by Cartoon Studios, Battle Creek, Michigan

Visit www.freddiefernortner.com

Printed in United States of America

First Printing - February 2007

THE MAGICAL
WADING POOL

VISIT CHILLERMANIA!

WORLD HEADQUARTERS FOR BOOKS BY JOHNATHAN RAND!

Yooperland

Indian River

Alpena

Traverse City

MICHIGAN

CHILLERMANIA!

**I-75 Exit 313
then south
1 mile!**

Mt. Pleasant   Bay City

Grand Rapids

Lansing

Kalamazoo   Detroit

Visit the HOME for books by Johnathan Rand! Featuring books, hats, shirts, bookmarks and other cool stuff not available anywhere else in the world! Plus, watch the American Chillers website for news of special events and signings at *CHILLERMANIA!* with author Johnathan Rand! Located in northern lower Michigan, on I-75! Take exit 313 . . . then south 1 mile! For more info, call (231) 238-0338. And be afraid! Be veeeery afraaaaaaiiiid . . . .

1

The day Freddie Fernortner's father brought home the magical wading pool was an exciting day, indeed. You see, Freddie, along with his best friends Darla and Chipper, had already had one big adventure: they had to save Freddie's cat, Mr. Chewy, from being carried away by a kite! Mr. Chewy got his name because, as a kitten, he learned how to chew gum and blow bubbles. And if you ever saw a cat chew gum and blow bubbles, you know just how funny it is!

The three first graders (and Freddie's cat, of course) were always looking for exciting things to do. Freddie Fernortner was very smart, and very fearless . . . which sometimes got the three friends in a lot of trouble.

And, once again, trouble wasn't far away.

Freddie, Darla, Chipper, and Mr. Chewy had been sitting on Freddie's porch when Mr. Fernortner came home carrying a box with bold letters that read:

CONTAINS ONE
MAGICAL WADING POOL

The three friends wasted no time tearing into the box to see what it was all about.

"A magical wading pool!" Freddie exclaimed. "I wonder what it does!"

"I don't know," Chipper said as he helped open the box. "But I bet it'll be fun!"

Inside the box was a blue inflatable pool, swim masks, and some strange looking, colorful rubber tubes. Darla picked one up and looked at it.

"What's this?" she wondered aloud.

"That's a snorkel," Freddie replied. "You use it to breathe while you float on the surface of the water. That way, you can look down through your mask and not have to take your face out of the water."

"It will be cool to have our very own pool to swim in!" Chipper said.

"Let's set it up in my back yard," Freddie said. "Come on. Let's put all this stuff back in the box and carry it around back."

The three first graders returned the masks and snorkels to the box. Then, they carefully placed the limp plastic pool inside, too. (Actually, it didn't look anything at all like a pool . . . not yet, anyway.)

All the while, Mr. Chewy watched from the porch, chewing gum and blowing bubbles.

The box wasn't very heavy, and the three friends had no trouble at all carrying it into the back yard. Now, all they had to do was find the perfect spot.

"I say we set it up over there," Freddie said as he pointed, "near the bird bath. That's a good, sunny spot."

"Sounds good to me," Chipper said.

"Me, too," chimed Darla.

They carried the big box into the yard next to the bird bath. The day was sunny and bright. The wind had been blowing earlier, and it had been quite gusty. Now, however, there was hardly any wind at all.

Chipper looked around. "Hey, Freddie," he said, "remember when we built that big box fort? That was a lot of fun!"

Freddie laughed. "Yeah," he said. "We should do that again sometime!"

Suddenly, Mrs. Fernortner's voice called out from the house. "Freddie! Time for dinner!"

"Okay, Mom," he replied. He was hungry . . . but he was a little disappointed. After all . . . he wanted to get right to work, setting up the magical wading pool.

"I guess we'll have to wait until tomorrow to set up our magical wading pool," he said. "Let's meet in the morning. Don't forget to wear your swim suit!"

"I don't get it," Darla said as she gazed at the pool. She had a puzzled look on her face. "What's so magical about it?"

It was a good question. Just what was so magical about the pool? Was it even magical at all?

Oh, you can bet it was . . . and Freddie, Darla, and Chipper would find out for themselves the very next day!

2

The next day was sunny, bright, and warm. The sky was a beautiful blue, and there were no clouds. The flowers in Mrs. Fernortner's garden soaked up the sunshine, while bumblebees flitted among the colorful petals.

Freddie, Chipper, and Darla met in Freddie's back yard. Mr. Chewy was there, too, and he sat by the bird bath, watching the three first graders. And, as usual, the cat was chewing gum and blowing bubbles.

"I was so excited last night I could hardly sleep!" Freddie said.

"Me, too!" Chipper said. "I've never been in a magical wading pool!"

The three first graders began to assemble the pool . . . which was pretty easy. All they had to do was take it out of the box (it looked like a big, blue bag that was folded) and blow it up. Freddie, Chipper, and Darla each took turns. Soon, the wading pool was ready. There was just one more thing they needed to do.

"Chipper, go get the hose from my mom's flower garden," Freddie said. "All we have to do is fill the pool with water, and we'll be ready."

Chipper hustled over to Mrs. Fernortner's garden and found the bright green water hose. He picked it up and carried it to the empty pool. While he did, Freddie ran to the house and turned the water on. Then, he ran back to the pool, where Darla and Chipper waited.

Water began running from the hose, and Freddie placed the end of it inside the wading pool. The water swirled and splashed as it filled the small wading pool.

But there was one small problem, and Darla was the first to notice it.

"The pool is very small, Freddie," she said. "If we try to swim, there won't be hardly any room."

Chipper scratched his head. "Gee, Freddie," he said. "Darla is right. The pool *is* really small."

Freddie agreed. "Yeah, it's small," he said. "But it will still be a lot of fun. And besides . . . the box says that it's magical."

"I haven't seen anything magical, yet," Darla said.

"Me neither," Chipper said.

True, the pool didn't look magical. There were no colorful decorations of fish or shells or anything. It was just a bright, plain blue.

In a few minutes, the pool was filled with water. Freddie ran back to the side of the house and turned the water off. Then he ran back to the pool. Darla and Chipper were staring down into the clean, clear water.

"It still doesn't look very magical," Darla said.

"Well, we have to give it a chance," Freddie said. And with that, he placed his foot in the water.

"Yipes!" he said, pulling his foot out quickly. "It's ice cold!"

Darla tried with her foot, and she, too,

pulled it out really fast. "You're right, Freddie," she said with a shiver. "It's freezing!"

"Let's wait for a while until the sun warms it up," Freddie said. "We'll freeze if we try and swim right now!"

The three first graders agreed to meet after lunch, in Freddie's back yard. That would give the sun plenty of time to warm the water in the magical wading pool.

"Very strange," Freddie said as he looked at the pool after Chipper and Darla had left. Mr. Chewy was still near the bird bath, chewing gum and blowing bubbles, but now he scampered up to the edge of the pool and looked into the water.

"It says it's a magical wading pool, Mr. Chewy," he said to his cat, "but it looks just like an ordinary wading pool."

But he was still excited about trying it out. That is, of course, when the water warmed up.

So, he went inside, where it was soon time for lunch. His mother made him a peanut butter and jelly sandwich. She also gave him an apple, several carrot sticks, and a glass of milk. She placed the meal on a tray, and Freddie carried it outside to the back yard patio, where he sat at the picnic table and ate. When he was finished, he took the tray back to the kitchen, thanked his mother, and went back outside. He sat down beneath a tree and waited for Darla and Chipper to arrive.

And, although Freddie didn't know it yet, the tiny wading pool was hard at work, becoming more and more magical by the moment.

3

"Freddie! Hey Freddie! Are you ready?"

It was Chipper. He was running across the grass, barefoot. Darla wasn't far behind him. Both children carried colorful beach towels.

Freddie stood. "Yeah!" he exclaimed. "Let's go!"

He got up, and the three first graders walked to the edge of the pool. Mr. Chewy had been sitting by Mrs. Fernortner's flower garden, watching bumblebees, and he, too, joined the children at the wading pool.

"Let's not forget the masks and snorkels," Chipper said.

Freddie went to the box and turned it upside down. Out came four masks and four snorkels.

"That's funny," Darla said. "There's a mask and snorkel for each of us, and one extra."

"Maybe Mr. Chewy would like to go," Chipper snickered.

"Hey, maybe he would!" Freddie said. Then he turned to Mr. Chewy. "Do you want to swim in the magical wading pool?" he asked.

"But Freddie," Darla interrupted, "Mr. Chewy can't swim."

"The pool is only a few inches deep," Freddie said. "He won't need to swim. He can just wade around with us."

Mr. Chewy seemed to like this idea. He scampered over to Mrs. Fernortner's garden, where he quickly dug a small hole in the dirt. He placed his wad of gum in the hole, then covered it up. (If Mrs. Fernortner knew he was doing this, she would not be very happy.) Then he ambled back to the waiting first graders.

"Let's see if this mask will fit you, Mr. Chewy," Freddie said. He slipped the mask over the cat's head. It was a perfect fit!

Darla laughed. "He looks funny!" she said as Freddie affixed the snorkel to Mr. Chewy's mask.

Then, the three first graders each put on a mask and clipped a snorkel to the strap.

"See, you put this end of the snorkel in your mouth, like this," Freddie said, showing Chipper and Darla. When he put it in his mouth is was hard for him to talk, but he managed. "That's how we can breathe while we look down in the water."

Chipper and Darla each put their snorkels into their mouths.

"I'm ready!" Chipper said, and his voice sounded hollow in the snorkel.

"I'm ready, too!" Darla said.

"We sound funny," Chipper said with a laugh. Mr. Chewy meowed in the snorkel, and he, too, sounded funny.

"Then, let's go!" Freddie said, placing a foot in the wading pool. The water was only deep enough to come up to his shin.

Then, he stepped all the way inside, and stood.

Darla stepped into the pool, and Chipper followed. Then, Mr. Chewy made a single, short leap . . . and landed in the pool. The water came up to his neck, but he didn't mind at all.

"So, where's the magic?" Chipper asked.

"I'm not feeling very magical," Darla said. "Maybe we got a broken wading pool."

"Maybe we have to swim around," Freddie said.

"Gee, there's not much room, with the three of us and Mr. Chewy," Chipper said.

"Well, let's give it a try," Freddie said, and he knelt down into the cool water.

Darla and Chipper knelt down, too.

"Just put your face in the water and breathe through your snorkel," Freddie said.

At the exact same time, the three first graders and Mr. Chewy leaned forward and placed their face masks into the water—and what they saw was *incredible*.

4

They were no longer in a wading pool! Beneath them was a vast sea, filled with brightly colored fish! There were rocks and plants and coral all around!

The three first graders were so stunned they pulled their faces from the water and drew back.

But when they looked into the pool, this is all they saw: the bottom of the pool!

"Did you see that?" Freddie spluttered through his snorkel.

"I saw all kinds of fish!" Chipper said.

"Me, too!" Darla exclaimed.

"It really *is* a magical wading pool, after all!" Freddie said.

"Do you think it's safe for kids?" Darla asked warily.

"Sure it is," Freddie said. "Or else they wouldn't sell them at the store. Besides, my dad wouldn't give us a pool that wasn't safe."

"Yeah, I guess you're right," Darla said.

"Let's do that again!" Chipper said eagerly. And with that, the three first graders plunged their faces into the water again.

It was hard to believe . . . but it was true! Beneath them, the wading pool had vanished. In every direction they looked, all they could see was a vast ocean, filled with undersea life.

In fact, the children were no longer kneeling in the pool, but freely floating on the surface of the water. Even Mr. Chewy had become an expert swimmer, and was having great fun trying to catch fish in his paws!

What's more, the three first graders found they could talk to one another while breathing through their snorkels. After all, that's what you'd expect from a magical wading pool!

A big, colorful fish swam right up to them, gave the three swimmers a curious look, and then swam off.

"Wow!" Chipper exclaimed. "He was cool!"

"There's another one!" Darla said, pointing at a big, orange and black fish that suddenly appeared. The fish swam by, not paying any attention to the three children and the cat swimming on the surface.

It was exciting, and it was fun. Freddie, Chipper, and Darla were having the time of their lives in the magical wading pool.

But some very strange things were about to happen . . . .

5

A school of yellow fish went by, and Mr. Chewy tried to catch one. He didn't succeed, but he sure tried hard!

"Freddie," Chipper said, "this has to be our best adventure yet!"

"Yeah!" Darla agreed. "This is so much fun!"

Beneath them, on the ocean floor, a giant stingray lumbered past. It was shaped like a triangle and had a long tail.

"I've seen things like this on television and in books," Freddie said, breathlessly. "But I've never seen anything like this for real!"

"Look at that big shell down there!" Chipper said, pointing. "I'm going to swim down for a closer look."

Suddenly, Chipper was needling down into the depths, expertly swimming through the crystal-blue waters.

"Hey, that looks like fun!" Darla said, and she, too, set off, following Chipper deep into the sea. Not to be left behind, Freddie followed, and even Mr. Chewy came along!

The bottom of the ocean was ablaze with all sorts of colorful things: fish, plants, shells, and coral.

"Look at the size of that shell!" Chipper said, and then he suddenly looked surprised.

"Did you guys hear that?" he asked Freddie and Darla.

"We sure did!" Freddie said. "We can talk, even when we're under water!"

"That's because it's magical!" Darla exclaimed. "I'm going to ask for a magical wading pool for my birthday!"

They took a moment and looked at the huge shell. It was almost bigger than they were!

"Let's swim over there," Freddie suggested, "by those rocks."

He started out, and the three first graders held hands as they swam. Mr. Chewy swam next to Freddie.

And all around them, the sea was teeming with life. Schools of fish were all around, and they paid no mind to the three first graders and the cat swimming among them.

"Look," Freddie said, pointing to a hole in a large rock. The hole was about the size of a basketball, but they couldn't see inside. It appeared to be a small cave of some sort.

"I'll bet a cool fish lives in there," Chipper said.

Chipper was wrong.

Oh, something lived there, all right. But it wasn't a fish.

As they watched, they saw something move in the hole.

Something was coming out.

Suddenly, all three first graders gasped in their snorkels.

Coming out of the hole was a sea snake!

6

Freddie didn't move. He couldn't . . . he was too frightened.

Chipper and Darla couldn't move, either. They were scared out of their wits. Even Mr. Chewy was frightened by the sight of the sea snake, which, by now, had come completely out of the hole and was directly in front of the three first graders, only a few feet away! He was white with black rings . . . or maybe he was black with white rings. It was impossible to tell for sure.

"Oh, what a day, what a day," the sea snake said, which confused the three first graders even more.

A talking sea snake? Freddie thought. *Sea snakes can't talk!*

But, then again, this was no ordinary wading pool. Like the box said: it was a *magical* wading pool. Strange, magical things were bound to happen.

"You . . . you can *talk?*" Chipper stammered.

"Of course I can," the sea snake replied. "I'm talking right now, aren't I?"

"But . . . but do you . . . do you *bite?*" Darla asked nervously.

"Of course I bite!" the sea snake replied.

"Do you bite little kids?" Freddie asked.

"Only if they bite me first," the sea snake replied, very matter-of-factly. Then, the snake eyed them warily. His eyes darted from Freddie, to Chipper, then to Darla. Then, back to Freddie. "You kids aren't going to bite me, are you?" the sea snake asked.

"Oh, no, no," Freddie replied quickly. "We're not here to bite anyone."

"Yeah, we're just here to explore," Chipper added. "We don't want to hurt anyone."

"Well, good, good," the sea snake hissed. "Say . . . I'm pretty hungry. You don't happen to have any pizza, do you?"

The three first graders looked at each other in disbelief.

"Pizza?!?!" Darla said.

"Yeah, pizza," the sea snake said. "I'm really hungry."

"Sea snakes eat pizza?!?!" Chipper exclaimed.

"Well, not all the time, we don't," the sea snake explained. "It just sounds good right now. Doesn't it?"

"We have some leftover pizza in the fridge," Freddie said. Which was true. The Fernortner's went out for pizza earlier in the week, and there were several pieces left over.

This caused the sea snake's eyes to light up. "Cold pizza?!?!" he exclaimed. "Can I have some? Pleeeeeeaaase?"

"Well, I guess I could go get a couple of slices," Freddie replied.

"I'll wait right here!" the sea snake said.

"I'll be right back," Freddie said to Chipper and Darla. "Don't go anywhere."

Freddie swam up to the surface. It was very strange: when he poked his head out of the water, he found that he was kneeling in the pool! The sea was gone! And right beside him, Darla, Chipper, and Mr. Chewy were leaning forward, peering into the pool, breathing through their snorkels!

Very strange.

But, he reminded himself as he leapt from the pool, *it's a magical wading pool. Anything is possible.*

He raced inside, not even taking the time to dry off. (If his mother would have known this, she would have thrown a fit . . . but she was in her sewing room, working on a shirt she'd been making.)

Freddie ran straight to the fridge and found two pieces of pizza wrapped in foil.

"Mom!" he called out. "I'm going to give the leftover pizza to a sea snake!"

But his mother didn't hear him over the

noise of the sewing machine.

Freddie removed the foil and tossed it into the garbage, then raced back to the pool with the slices of cold pizza.

Chipper, Darla, and Mr. Chewy were still in the pool, staring down.

Freddie leapt back into the pool. As soon as his mask touched the water, he was in the sea again! Chipper, Darla, and Mr. Chewy were now below him, talking to the sea snake!

It was very, very strange.

Freddie swam down, carrying the pizza in one hand. Which was difficult, because the pizza became very soft and gooey in the water.

The sea snake was delighted. "Oh, my, delicious, delicious!" he exclaimed. "I can't wait!"

Freddie held out the two slices of pizza, and the sea snake quickly gobbled them up.

"Ah! Pepperoni! My favorite!" the sea snake said, after he'd swallowed both pieces in a single gulp. "Wonderful! Thank you!"

"You're welcome," Freddie said.

"Now, if you don't mind," the sea snake said, "I think I'll take a nap. All this eating has made me tired. You kids try not to make too much noise, okay? A sea snake needs his sleep, you know."

Before the first graders could answer, the sea snake sank back into its home, where it vanished.

"Well, that was unusual," Darla said. "I've never seen a talking snake."

"Or, one that eats pizza," Freddie added. "He seemed nice enough, though."

"Guys," Chipper said, "do . . . do you think everything in here is nice?" He sounded nervous.

"I don't know," Freddie said. "Why?"

"Well, I saw an electric eel on television once, and it didn't look very nice." Chipper's voice was tense, and he sounded scared.

"Really?" Darla asked. "You saw one on television? What did it look like?"

Slowly, Chipper pointed, and his hand was trembling. "It looked just like that one . . . right behind you!"

7

Freddie and Darla spun, but their movements were slow and sluggish in the water.

But Chipper was right! Behind them was an electric eel . . . and he was twice as big as the sea snake! The eel was a golden brown color with tan spots, and his head was bigger and rounder than the snake's. The eel also had two gills, just behind its head.

Freddie, Darla, and Chipper—even Mr.

Chewy—were shocked. (Well, not really shocked in an electrical sense, as the electric eel meant them no harm.)

"You're . . . you're an electric eel!" Freddie stammered.

"You were expecting a unicorn?" the eel said. "Of *course* I'm an electric eel. And right now, I'm not a very happy eel."

"What's wrong?" Darla asked.

"It's my parents," the eel said, shaking his head. "They grounded me until the next high tide."

"Grounded?" Chipper asked. "Why?"

"I got caught in the wrong current and swam too far from home. Mom and Dad got mad. They grounded me!"

An electric eel that's grounded because of a current? Freddie wondered. *My, what a strange magical wading pool this is.*

"Well, I'm sorry you're grounded," Chipper said, "but we don't have the power to do anything."

"Oh, I know," the electric eel said with a sigh. "It's my own fault. I tried to tell them that once I was caught in the current, I didn't have the energy to swim back. I guess that'll teach me."

"That's a bummer," Freddie said.

All of a sudden, the electric eel's eyes grew very large. He looked frightened. Without warning, he shuddered, turned, and swam off in a hurry.

"What was that all about?" Darla asked. "He sure got spooked."

The three first graders, along with Mr. Chewy, were watching the electric eel fade into the distance . . . and they didn't see the school of barracuda sneaking up behind them.

8

"I wonder what could have scared him away like that," Freddie said.

Then, at the exact same time, the three first graders felt something was very wrong . . . and whatever it was, they realized it was right behind them.

They all turned to see four huge barracudas staring at them, their sharp teeth gleaming.

Freddie, Chipper, and Darla were so scared they couldn't move. Mr. Chewy closed his eyes. They knew there was no escape from the terrible fish.

Then, one of the barracudas spoke.

"Knock, knock," he said.

"Uh . . . what was that?" Freddie stammered.

"Knock, knock," the barracuda repeated.

Freddie was confused. "Um, what—"

"Oh, for goodness' sake!" the fish said, somewhat annoyed. "It's a knock-knock joke! Knock, knock!"

"Who . . . who's there?" Chipper said, his voice shaking.

"Barra," the fish replied.

"Barra-who?" Darla said.

"Barra-with me a moment, I think I'm going to sneeze!"

At this, all four barracudas broke into a fit of laughter.

"Get it? Get it?" the barracuda said. "Barra-with me? Clever, huh?"

"Yeah, I guess so," Freddie said. Actually, he thought the joke was corny, but he didn't mind. He was just glad he wasn't barracuda lunch!

"Here's another one," another barracuda said. "Knock, knock."

"Who's there?" Freddie, Chipper, and Darla said at the same time.

"Dwayne," the barracuda replied.

"Dwayne who?" the three first graders asked.

"Dwayne the water from this ocean, and we're all goners!" the barracuda said, and all four fish were once again pitching with laughter.

"*Gee . . . they aren't even very funny,*" Chipper whispered. "*My dad has better jokes than these!*"

The barracudas continued their laughter, and slowly swam away, telling each other knock-knock jokes.

"This sure is a strange wading pool, Freddie," Chipper said. "I've never seen anything like it!"

"I wonder what we'll see next," Darla said.

"I don't know," Freddie replied, "but I'm having a lot of fun! Let's swim some more and see what else we can discover!" The three friends, along with Mr. Chewy, continued swimming. They marveled at the colorful fish and plant life. It truly was like being in a totally different world.

"Look at that big rock," Darla said,

pointing. "It's all shiny and smooth."

Chipper and Freddie turned to see what Darla was pointing at.

But do you think it was a rock she was pointing at?

You're right. It *wasn't* a rock—and were they ever surprised to discover what it really was!

9

Once again, Freddie, Chipper, Darla, and Mr. Chewy were taken completely by surprise.

What they were looking at wasn't a rock—it was a giant sea turtle! He was mostly green, and he was very, very large. In fact, his head was bigger than a bowling ball!

The turtle swam up to the three first graders.

"I don't suppose you folks want a ride

anywhere, do you?" the turtle asked.

"What do you mean?" Freddie replied.

"You know . . . a ride. I'm a taxi turtle. If you need a ride somewhere, I can take you."

"Really?" Darla said.

"That's my job," the turtle said. "It's a tough job, but some turtle has to do it."

"Hey, that might be kind of fun!" Chipper said. "I've never ridden on the back of a turtle before!"

"Climb on," the turtle said. "I'll take you around and show you the sights."

"Wow!" Freddie exclaimed as the three first graders climbed atop the turtle's shell. Mr. Chewy climbed on, too.

"Hang on," the taxi turtle said, and he began swimming deeper and deeper.

"Wait until I tell my mom and dad about this!" Darla said. "This is so much fun!"

The turtle swam all around the sea and showed them many interesting things. Freddie, Chipper, and Darla learned a lot about the ocean and sea life.

Soon, however, the turtle slowed to a stop. "Okay, end of the ride," he said. "That'll be twenty clams."

Freddie looked at Chipper. Chipper looked at Darla. Darla looked at Freddie. The three first graders looked very puzzled.

"Twenty clams?" Freddie replied.

"Well, you don't think I do this for free, do you?" the turtle huffed.

Freddie was confused. "Well, I, uh, I guess that—"

"Cough it up, bud," the turtle said. "Twenty clams."

"We don't have any clams," Chipper said. "We don't even have pockets in our swimsuits."

The turtle looked like he was getting angry.

"Wait," Freddie said. "We have some apples, and my mom has some vegetables growing in the garden. They're very tasty."

At this, the turtle perked up. "Apples?" he said. "I *love* apples!"

"Do sea turtles eat apples?" Darla whispered to Chipper.

"I don't know," Chipper whispered back, *"but this one does."*

"I'll be right back!" Freddie said. "Wait here!"

Once again, he swam off. And, once again, when he reached the surface, he was surprised to see Darla, Chipper, and Mr. Chewy kneeling in the water, peering into the pool with their face masks on, breathing through their snorkels.

First, he ran into his house to retrieve the apples. Again, he didn't take the time to dry off. He needed to get the apples to the turtle—*fast!*

He grabbed the last two apples from the counter.

"Hey Mom!" Freddie called out. "I'm giving some apples and green beans to a big sea turtle!"

But his mother, who was still busy sewing in another room, didn't hear him.

Then, Freddie went outside, where he sprinted to his mother's garden. There, he found lots of big, healthy green beans. He picked as many as he could carry, and hustled back to the wading pool. Stepping into the water, he knelt down, and peered into the pool with his face mask.

And there was the sea again! Right below him, his friends were waiting . . . and so was the sea turtle.

Freddie swam down and gave the food to the turtle, who quickly began gobbling it up.

Chipper, Darla, and Mr. Chewy just watched. They didn't know what to think of the huge turtle before them, gobbling up the apples and green beans.

While he was eating, they heard a sudden, shrill ringing noise. Freddie, Chipper, and Darla were alarmed . . . but not the sea turtle. He reached down with one of his flippers and pulled a small telephone from his shell.

"Taxi turtle," he said into the phone. "Uh-huh. Fine. Be right there." Then, he put the phone back into his shell, and looked at the three first graders.

"Sorry to eat and run," he said, "but some lobster needs a ride home from the sand bar. Thanks for the grub."

The big turtle turned and swam off while the three first graders watched.

"Okay, that does it," Freddie said. "There's no way things can get any stranger."

But they were about to. In fact, things were about to get a whole *lot* stranger.

10

Freddie, Chipper, Darla, and Mr. Chewy had never had an experience like this before.

But, then again, they'd never played in a magical wading pool before, either. Here, everything was exciting and new and wonderful. They never knew what was going to happen, or what they would see next. It was fun.

They were swimming idly along,

watching fish, when all of a sudden a flash of black and white shot past them like a torpedo! Then, another zipped by, leaving a trail of white, foaming bubbles!

"What were those things?!?!" Chipper asked.

"I don't know," Freddie replied, "but they sure do move fast!"

Zoom! One of them went past again, very fast, followed by the other one.

"Hey!" Darla exclaimed, "I know what those are! Those are penguins!"

"Penguins?!?!" Freddie replied. "What are *they* doing here?"

"It's a magical wading pool, Freddie," Chipper said. "Remember? Anything can happen!"

The two creatures whirled past again, like they were totally unaware of the three first graders. Then, one of them slowed, circled a few times, and stopped in front of them. The second penguin stopped, too.

"My, what strange looking fish you are," one penguin said. "What kind of fish are you?"

"We're not fish!" Darla huffed, clearly upset by the remark.

"We're kids," Chipper said.

"We're penguins," one of the penguins said, "and we're lost. Can you point us in the direction of the South Pole?"

Freddie looked at Darla, and Darla looked at Chipper. Chipper looked at Freddie. The three first graders didn't know, and all they could do was shrug.

"We don't know," Freddie admitted. "We just went swimming in our magical wading pool. We have no idea which way south is."

"Oh, dear," one of the penguins said. "It looks like we'll be late for the birthday party, after all."

Suddenly, both penguins looked very sad, and the three first graders wanted to do something to help.

"Isn't there anything we can do?" Darla asked.

"I'm afraid," one of the penguins said, "if we don't know our way south, we'll never it make it home."

Suddenly, Freddie had an idea. "My dad has a compass!" he exclaimed. "It will tell you what direction to go! I'll get it for you!"

And with that, Freddie was once again on his way to the surface, where he stepped out of the pool and raced to his house.

"Mom!" Freddie shouted as he went into the kitchen. "I'm going to give Dad's compass to two penguins, so they can find their way to the south pole!"

But Freddie's mom was upstairs, running the vacuum . . . and she didn't hear him.

Freddie pulled open the top kitchen drawer and found his father's compass. It was a little bigger than a quarter, and made of strong plastic. Holding it tightly in his hand, he ran outside and leapt into the pool . . . where he found Chipper, Darla, Mr. Chewy, and the two penguins waiting for him.

"Got it!" he said proudly, and he handed the compass to one of the penguins. The penguin had a difficult time holding the device, because he didn't have fingers, he had wings. But he managed.

Freddie explained how to use it, and soon, the penguins knew in which direction they needed to go.

"Make sure you check the compass often," Freddie said, "so you stay on course!"

"Thank you, thank you," the penguins said. "When we get to the South Pole, we'll send you a postcard!"

In a flash, the penguins had zipped away, leaving only a cloud of bubbles that quickly began to rise to the surface.

"A postcard from the South Pole?" Darla said. "Penguins don't have postcards!"

"Or stamps," Chipper said.

"They do in the magical wading pool," Freddie said.

"I'll bet it's going to take them a long time to get to where they're going," Chipper said. "That was really nice of you to give them your dad's compass."

"Speaking of a long time," Freddie said, "we've been in the pool a long time. We should probably get out and take a break. Besides . . . I can't wait to tell Mom all about our adventure!"

The three first graders and Mr. Chewy were about to swim to the surface . . . but it wasn't going to be that easy.

You see, right at that very moment, a dark shadow fell over them.

They looked up . . . only to see the biggest, meanest-looking great white shark ever to swim the ocean.

11

Up until now, the adventure in the magical wading pool had been fun. Sure, there had been a couple of scary moments, but nothing bad had happened.

Now, however, with the giant, great white shark coming toward them, the three first graders—and Mr. Chewy, too—were more frightened than they'd ever been in their lives. Why, this was even scarier than crashing Freddie's flying bicycle! It was scarier than the time they went looking for a super-scary night thingy. And it was even scarier than the time they visited a haunted house.

And the shark kept coming closer and closer.

Someone started to sniffle and cry.

It wasn't Freddie.

It wasn't Chipper.

It wasn't Darla, nor was it Mr. Chewy.

It was the great white shark! The shark was crying!

The giant beast stopped right in front of the three first graders. Freddie, Chipper, and Darla were still very afraid . . . but the shark didn't look like it was going to hurt them. In fact, it seemed sad. It was sniffling and crying and carrying on terribly.

Finally, Freddie got up the courage to speak.

"What's . . .what's wrong, Mr. Shark?" he stammered. He was a little nervous, since it wasn't everyday he found himself face to face with a great white shark!

"Oh me, oh my, whatever am I going to do?" the shark said. "What am I going to do?"

"About what?" Chipper asked.

"My teeth," the shark replied, and he let out with a terrible sob.

"What's wrong with them?" Darla asked.

"Nothing, yet," the great white shark replied. "But I've lost my toothbrush, and now I have no way to clean them! This is horrible!"

"Sharks use toothbrushes?!?!" Freddie exclaimed.

"Of course we do!" the shark replied sharply. "We're the fiercest creatures in the ocean! We have to keep our teeth sharp and clean! I have an image to keep up, you know. If people don't see my clean, sharp teeth, they won't be afraid of me anymore. I'll be out of a job!"

"What job is that?" Darla asked.

"I do security at a couple of coral reefs," the shark sniffed. "It pays the bills, until something better comes along."

"Do you remember where you last had your toothbrush?" Freddie asked.

"No," the shark sniffed.

"Don't worry," Freddie said, "just wait here." Once again, Freddie left the magical wading pool and went into his house. He went into the bathroom and found his toothbrush, but it wasn't very big. His dad's was bigger . . . so he took it, instead.

From the kitchen, he called out to his mother: "Mom! I'm giving dad's toothbrush to a great white shark!"

But his mother was in the laundry room, and the dryer was running. Over the noise, she couldn't hear him.

Deep within the magical wading pool, Chipper, Darla, Mr. Chewy, and the great white shark were waiting patiently. Freddie returned, and he handed the toothbrush to the shark, who curled his fin around it.

"Oh, thank you, thank you, thank you!" the shark repeated. "I am so thankful."

"You're welcome," Freddie said, and the shark began brushing his teeth as he slipped slowly into the deep sea.

"I can't believe we just talked to a great white shark!" Chipper said.

"Yeah," Darla agreed. "He was scary, at first. But I didn't know that sharks brushed their teeth. Were you scared, too, Freddie?"

But Freddie wasn't listening.

"Freddie?" Darla repeated. "Weren't you scared?"

Still, Freddie didn't answer. He was

motionless, staring down into the depths of the sea. Colorful fish flitted all around him.

Darla and Chipper became worried. Mr. Chewy was worried.

"Freddie!" Chipper exclaimed. "Is something wrong?!?! Are you all right?!?!"

"Chipper!" Darla shrieked. "What's happening?!?! Freddie! *Freddie!*"

12

"Freddie!" Darla called out again. "Freddie! Freddie, are you ready?!?!"

Freddie Fernortner opened his eyes. He was confused. Someone had been calling his name . . . .

He looked around. He was laying in the grass, and Mr. Chewy was next to him. Above, the big tree cast its shadow over him. Not far away, by the bird bath, the blue wading pool waited, its water glimmering in the afternoon sun.

Darla and Chipper ran up to him. They were wearing their swim suits and carrying beach towels.

"Are you ready?!?!" Chipper asked.

"I . . . I guess so," Freddie said. "I must have fallen asleep."

Then, he suddenly remembered everything: the fish, the turtle, the school of barracudas that told knock-knock jokes. He remembered the sea snake and the electric eel and the great white shark.

"You . . . you mean it was all a dream?" Freddie asked his friends.

"What dream?" Darla asked, and Freddie told her and Chipper all about the strange dream he had about the magical wading pool.

"That was some dream!" Chipper said, when Freddie had finished. "That would be a lot of fun!"

"Let's go see if it works!" Darla said, and

the three first graders donned the masks and snorkels. Mr. Chewy decided to sit next to the pool and watch.

Freddie placed a single foot in the wading pool. Then, he stepped all the way in.

"I'll look first," he said, and he knelt down.

He placed his face mask into the water.

The only thing he saw was the bottom of the pool, inches away.

In a way, he was a little disappointed. He'd really hoped the wading pool really *was* magical, that he and Chipper and Darla would be able to swim around the sea and meet strange and interesting creatures.

He stood up and shook his head. "Nope," he said. "Nothing but the bottom of the pool."

Darla stepped in, followed by Chipper. They splashed and laughed and had a lot of fun in the magical wading pool, that turned out to be not-so-magical.

But Freddie got to thinking.

You know, he thought, *I have my three best friends with me, right now: Darla, Chipper, and Mr. Chewy. We're having a lot of fun together. What can be more magical than that?*

They played in the pool for a long, long time, until Chipper and Darla had to go home.

"See you tomorrow, Freddie," Darla said. "I hope we can play in your magical wading pool again."

"Yeah!" Chipper replied. "Thanks, Freddie! That was a lot of fun!"

"We'll play again tomorrow," Freddie said, and he dried himself off as his two friends walked home.

"Come on, Mr. Chewy," Freddie said to his cat. "Time to go inside."

Now remember: all this time, Freddie thought his strange experience earlier in the day had been a dream.

But something really weird was about to happen . . . .

13

During dinner (which happened to be roast chicken and dumplings, one of Freddie's favorites), Freddie told his mother and father all about the magical wading pool.

But he didn't tell them about his dream.

His father talked about taking a vacation, and his mother agreed that it would be a good idea. They talked about all the fun places they could go.

"You know," Freddie's dad said as they were just finishing dinner. "I can't seem to find my toothbrush anywhere. I looked and looked, but it's gone. And my compass is missing from the kitchen drawer."

Mrs. Fernortner frowned. "And I'm missing a bunch of green beans from my garden. And I can't find the three apples I was saving, or the leftover pizza that was in the fridge."

Freddie looked dazed.

"Do you know where they went, Freddie?" his mother asked.

Freddie looked very sheepish, and he glanced down at the floor. "Yes," he said very quietly.

His mother and father looked at him.

"Well?" his father said. "Where did those things go?"

Freddie took a breath, and then spoke.

"Let's see," he began. "I gave the pizza to a sea snake who was hungry. I gave the apples and the beans to a turtle, because we didn't have any clams to pay him for giving us a ride. Then, I gave the compass to two penguins who were lost and on their way to a birthday party at the South Pole. And then, I gave Dad's toothbrush to a great white shark who'd lost his, and said he needed to keep his teeth clean for his security job at the coral reef."

When he was finished explaining, he looked at his parents, expecting to be in a whole lot of trouble.

But his mother and father just stared at him.

Then they burst out laughing, and began cleaning up the dinner dishes. "Freddie

Fernortner," his mother said, "you have the wildest imagination I have ever seen!"

Freddie just shrugged. His parents never again asked him where the pizza, apples, beans, compass, and toothbrush went.

The next day was cloudy and rainy, so the three first graders would have to wait to play in the magical wading pool. Freddie walked over to Chipper's house, where he found him in the garage, trying to fix an old wagon. Darla arrived at the same time, and the three began discussing fun things they could do. After all . . . there still was a lot of summer left.

"You know what would be fun," Chipper said excitedly, "is our very own carnival!"

"A carnival?!?!" chirped Darla. "What do you mean?"

"You know, like the ones they have at school! We could have one in my back yard! We could make up games for people to play, and we could even sell tickets!"

"That would be a blast!" Freddie said. "I bet we'd make a lot of money!"

"Do you want to do it?" Chipper asked.

"I do!" Freddie said quickly.

"Me, too!" Darla exclaimed. "Let's have a carnival! What do we do first?"

Chipper thought about it. "Well," he said, "first, we need a plan."

"Plans are good," Freddie said.

"Let's get started!" Darla cried. "Oh boy! Our very own carnival!"

And that was that. The three first graders—Freddie, Chipper, and Darla—were about to turn the whole neighborhood upside down!

NEXT:
FREDDIE FERNORTNER,
FEARLESS FIRST GRADER

BOOK EIGHT:

CHIPPER'S CRAZY CARNIVAL

CONTINUE ON TO READ
THE FIRST CHAPTER FOR
FREE!

1

Freddie Fernortner was excited, and he had a good reason to be. You see, Freddie and his pals, Chipper and Darla, had come up with a great way to earn some money. Best of all, it would be a lot of fun.

Chipper was the one who had the idea first. He had come up with the idea of having a carnival in his back yard. People could play fun games and win prizes. Everyone would have a great time.

Even Mr. Chewy, Freddie's cat, seemed to be excited. Mr. Chewy got his name because he liked to chew gum and blow bubbles. He was a good cat, too, and he followed Freddie everywhere he went. Mr. Chewy was the kind of cat any girl or boy would want to have as a friend.

One morning, Freddie woke up and dressed very quickly. This was the day that he, Chipper, and Darla would meet to make plans for their carnival.

While Freddie was eating his bowl of cereal, his mother came into the kitchen.

"Guess what?" Freddie said, nearly shouting. He was, after all, very excited.

"What?" his mother asked.

"Me and Chipper and Darla are going to have a carnival in Chipper's back yard!" he said as he scooped another spoonful of cereal out of the bowl.

"That sounds fun," his mother said with smile.

"It will be!" Freddie said.

"Don't talk with your mouth full," his mother reminded him.

Freddie finished chewing and swallowed. "We're going to have a blast!" he said. "And, we're going to earn money, too!"

"It sounds like it will be a lot of work," his mother said.

Freddie shook his head. "No, it wont!" he replied. "It'll be easy! We're going to make plans and figure everything out today!"

However, plans don't always work out the way you want them to.

Do you think it would be easy for Freddie, Chipper, and Darla to have a carnival in Chipper's back yard.

Maybe.

Do you think everything would go as planned?

Not hardly!

Freddie, Darla, and Chipper were about to find out that their plan wasn't going to go as planned at all. In fact, some of the things that would happen were going to be quite scary.

So, if you get scared easily, you might not want to read any more of this story. It might just be better for you to put the book down and find another one.

But if you think you're brave, and you want to find out what happened to Freddie, Chipper, Darla, and Mr. Chewy, then turn the page . . . .

ABOUT THE AUTHOR

Johnathan Rand is the author of more than 50 books, with well over 2 million copies in print. Series include **AMERICAN CHILLERS, MICHIGAN CHILLERS, FREDDIE FERNORTNER, FEARLESS FIRST GRADER**, and **THE ADVENTURE CLUB**. He's also co-authored a novel for teens (with Christopher Knight) entitled **PANDEMIA**. When not traveling, Rand lives in northern Michigan with his wife and two dogs. He is also the only author in the world to have a store that sells only his works: **CHILLERMANIA!** is located in Indian River, Michigan. Johnathan Rand is not always at the store, but he has been known to drop by frequently. Find out more at:

www.americanchillers.com

WATCH FOR MORE
FREDDIE FERNORTNER,
FEARLESS FIRST GRADER
BOOKS, COMING SOON!